CAPTAIN JIRI
and RABBI JACOB

CAPTAIN JIRI

and RABBI JACOB

adapted from
a Jewish folktale
and illustrated by
MARILYN HIRSH

Holiday House · New York

Library of Congress Cataloging in Publication Data
Hirsh, Marilyn.
    Captain Jiri and Rabbi Jacob.

    SUMMARY: Because their guardian angels get
confused, a scholarly rabbi and a pugnacious captain
meet and gain new insights into solving their
problems.
    [1. Folklore, Jewish]   I. Title.
PZ8.1.H66Cap   [398.2] [E]   76-6114
ISBN 0-8234-0279-7

TO EUGENE, ROSE, ALAN, GRETCHEN,
MICHAEL, VICKI, CARLA, AND ERIC.

Long ago, in the city of Cracow, there lived an old rabbi named Jacob. He was so good that the neighbors said, "He's an angel from heaven." The children were always creeping up behind him to look for his wings, but they could never find them.

At the same time, in the city of Prague, there lived a brave, strong soldier named Captain Jiri. His job was to guard the main bridge that led into the city. When the good people saw him, they felt safe, but the bad people were afraid and ran away.

Rabbi Jacob's house was filled with old books. The children came to study and learn about the laws of God and man. In a corner, the old men argued about the very same laws. Some discussions went on for days, but everybody loved to argue so it did not matter.

For years, Captain Jiri led his men up and down over the bridge.
Through snow and sleet or on the hottest summer days, he and his
soldiers protected the people of Prague. They were always ready to fight,
even if it wasn't necessary.

But Captain Jiri and his men were all the sons of poor peasants. They could not read or write and only knew how to be good soldiers. At night, when they finished work, they began to drink. After awhile, some would fall asleep and some would fight. Captain Jiri felt that there must be a better way to live, but he didn't know what it was.

Rabbi Jacob had his troubles too. On the way to
and from his house, his students were often chased
by bullies from other neighborhoods. The children
were used to studying and did not know how to pro-
tect themselves. Rabbi Jacob worried about the children's safety. He looked through his old books and
found answers to many strange and wonderful ques-
tions. But he did not find anything that would help
him keep the children safe.

One night, a guardian angel, dressed like Captain Jiri, appeared to Rabbi Jacob. "In the city of Prague, under the main bridge, there is a great treasure," the angel announced. "This treasure is for you." Without realizing that he had visited the wrong person, the angel disappeared.

On the very same night, a guardian angel, dressed like Rabbi Jacob, appeared to Captain Jiri. "In the city of Cracow, in the house of Rabbi Jacob, there is a great treasure," the angel announced. "This treasure is for you." Without realizing that he too had visited the wrong person, the angel disappeared.

It is not right to ignore an angel, so early the next morning, Rabbi Jacob set out for Prague. At the same time, Captain Jiri set out for Cracow. The road was filled with knights and ladies, with farmers, jugglers, merchants, and beggars. The trip was exciting but very long and tiring. Rabbi Jacob had to stop and rest along the way, but Captain Jiri marched steadily on without getting tired. They passed each other on the road without even knowing it.

Rabbi Jacob finally arrived in Prague. He easily found the main bridge. However, all that he found under the bridge was water. He noticed the soldiers of Captain Jiri's company. "If only my students looked like that, no one would bother them," he thought. After three days of looking under, over, and around the bridge, Rabbi Jacob decided to go home. "That was a funny-looking angel," he thought. "It was probably just a dream."

Captain Jiri had a hard time finding Rabbi Jacob's house, but he finally did. He went inside and started looking around. The children and old men were so busy arguing that they did not even notice him. Captain Jiri was glad to hear the students arguing about ideas instead of fighting and drinking. "If only my soldiers could learn to argue like that," he thought. Captain Jiri did not find his treasure and decided to go home. "That angel was pretty funny-looking," he thought. "Maybe I was just seeing things."

Rabbi Jacob and Captain Jiri both started on the long road home. But as they were passing one another, they noticed something strange. They stopped and stared at each other.

"You look like an angel," said Captain Jiri.

"Well, so do you," said Rabbi Jacob.

Just then, the guardian angels appeared. "In the city of Prague, under the main bridge, there is great treasure," announced the angel who looked like Captain Jiri. "This treasure is for you."

"For me?" asked Rabbi Jacob and Captain Jiri together.

"Do not interrupt angels," said the angels.

"In the city of Cracow, in the house of Rabbi Jacob, there is a great treasure," announced the other angel, who looked like Rabbi Jacob. "This treasure is for you."

"For me?" Rabbi Jacob and Captain Jiri cried again.

"We have said this all twice now," declared the guardian angels together, and disappeared into a passing cloud.

Rabbi Jacob and Captain Jiri watched them go in amazement, and then looked at each other. They began to smile as they realized that even guardian angels can make mistakes. In a moment they said good-bye and hurried to their own homes.

Rabbi Jacob had always wondered about a little door high up in the top of the fireplace. He stood on a stool and opened the door. Out came a lot of dust and a big bag full of gold coins.

Captain Jiri knew about a big loose stone under the bridge. "I'm sure that's the spot for a treasure," he thought. And he was right! As soon as the stone was pulled out, the soldiers could see bright gold coins in a big bag.

Rabbi Jacob remembered the soldiers and how brave they looked. With his treasure, he bought the children uniforms with bright red hats. He hired an old soldier to teach them how to defend themselves. Soon their cheeks turned pink and their eyes were bright. The next time the bullies came, the students yelled and made their scariest faces. They chased the bullies out of the neighborhood, and they did not come back. Rabbi Jacob and the children agreed that it was healthy to defend themselves, and they should make it part of their studies from then on.

Captain Jiri remembered the books and discussions in Rabbi Jacob's house. He used his treasure to buy books and hired an old scholar to teach the soldiers to read. One soldier learned to write poetry and another to play the lute. One became a fine artist while another knitted long socks of his own design. One preferred to continue drinking and did so.

Captain Jiri and Rabbi Jacob met every so often to discuss their experiences with angels. Captain Jiri advised Rabbi Jacob on training the children, and Rabbi Jacob brought Captain Jiri some new books to read. They were happy that their guardian angels had made a mistake, or they would not have become friends.